Red
is
Best

Twenty-fifth printing, August 2000

Annick Press Ltd.

We acknowledge the support of the Canada Council for the Arts, the Ontario
Arts Council, and the Government of Canada through the Book Publishing
Industry Development Program (BPIDP) for our publishing activities.

Cataloging in Publication Data
  Stinson, Kathy.
    Red is best

(Annick toddler series)
ISBN 0-920236-24-3 (bound).—ISBN 0-920236-26-X (pbk.)

I. Lewis, Robin Baird. II. Title. III. Series.

PS8587.T56R42 1982 jC813'.54 C82-094732-6
PZ7.S74Re

Distributed in Canada by:
Firefly Books Ltd.
3680 Victoria Park Avenue
Willowdale, ON
M2H 3K1

Published in the U.S.A. by Annick Press (U.S.) Ltd.
Distributed in the U.S.A. by:
Firefly Books (U.S.) Inc.
P.O. Box 1338
Ellicott Station
Buffalo, NY 14205

Printed and bound in Canada by
Friesens, Altona, Manitoba.

visit us at: **www.annickpress.com**

Red
is
Best

Story
Kathy Stinson

Art
Robin Baird Lewis

Annick Press Ltd.
Toronto • New York • Vancouver

My mom doesn't understand about red.

I like my red stockings the best.

My mom says, "Wear these. Your white stockings
look good with that dress."

But I can jump higher in my red stockings.

I like my red stockings the best.

I like my red jacket the best.

My mom says, "You need to wear your blue jacket.
It's too cold out for your red jacket."

But how can I be Red Riding Hood in my blue jacket?

I like my red jacket the best.

I like my red boots the best.

My mom says, "You can't
wear your red boots
in the snow. They're just
for rainy weather."

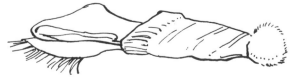

But my red boots take bigger steps.

I like my red boots the best.

I like my red mitts the best.

My mom says, "Your brown mitts are warmer. Your red mitts have holes in them."

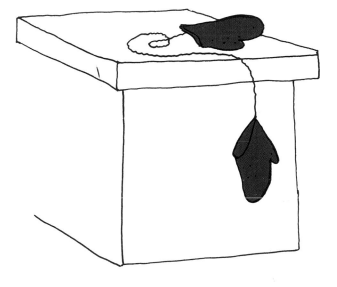

But my red mitts make better snowballs.

I like my red mitts best.

My mom says, ''Your yellow pyjamas will keep you warm
when you kick off your blankets.''

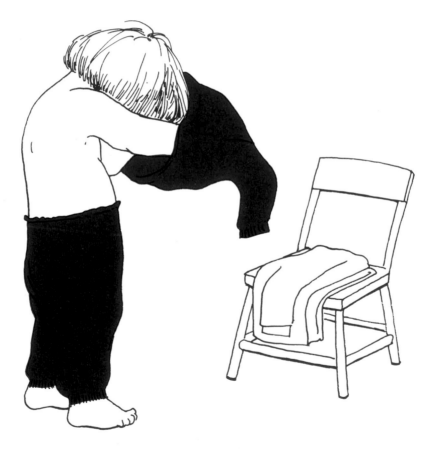

But my red pyjamas keep the monsters away
when I'm sleeping. I like my red pyjamas the best.

I like the red cup the best.

My mom says, "Oh, Kelly, what difference does it make?
I already poured it in the green cup."

But juice tastes better in the red cup.

I like the red cup best.

I like my red barrettes the best.

My mom says, "You wear pink barrettes with a pink dress."

But my red barrettes make my hair laugh.

I like my red barrettes best.

I like red paint the best.

My mom says, "But, Kelly, there is hardly any red paint left.
Maybe you could use orange instead."

But red paint puts singing in my head.

I like the red paint best.

I like red, because red is best.